ANH DO

ILLUSTRATED BY
DAN McGUINESS

HOT DOG! 14

TIDY TIME!

A Scholastic Press book
from Scholastic Australia

Scholastic Press
An imprint of Scholastic Australia Pty Limited (ABN 11 000 614 577)
PO Box 579 Gosford NSW 2250
www.scholastic.com.au

Part of the Scholastic Group
Sydney • Auckland • New York • Toronto • London • Mexico City
• New Delhi • Hong Kong • Buenos Aires • Puerto Rico

First published by Scholastic Australia in 2023.
Text copyright © Anh Do, 2023.
Illustrations by Dan McGuiness, copyright © Scholastic Australia, 2023.
Cover and internal design by Nicole Stofberg and Grace Felstead.

A catalogue record for this
book is available from the
National Library of Australia

ISBN: 978-1-76112-742-7

Typeset in YWFT Mullino.

Printed in China by Hang Tai Printing Company Limited.
Scholastic Australia's policy, in association with Hang Tai,
is to use papers that are renewable and made efficiently from wood grown
in responsibly managed forests, so as to minimise its environmental footprint.

10 9 8 7 6 5 4 3 2 1   23 24 25 26 27 / 2

ONE

Hey everyone, I'm **Hotdog!**

SPOT ANY RUBBISH?

This is my friend, **Lizzie.**

I'M JUST LEARNING –
I'M PICKING IT UP
AS I GO!

And this is our best buddy, **Kev.**

Today is **Tidy Your Town Day!** We are ready to roam around town with rubbish bags to help clean up our planet!

Everyone is joining in. This place is going to be spotless – except for our garbage bags, of course!

Plus, whoever collects the most bags of rubbish on the day wins a **GIANT JUNGLE HOLIDAY!**

Not **THAT** kind of **GIANT** jungle!

THIS kind of giant jungle!

We woke up **REALLY** early this morning and got ready to go. We had a **BIG** day ahead.

Kev even had a surprise for us all!

Those grabby tools made picking up rubbish **SO** much easier!

We were collecting rubbish **SO FAST!**
We were reaching, grabbing and
flinging trash into our bags.

Kev even found a slinky.

THIS IS WHAT I CALL *SPRING* CLEANING!

Our bags were filling up fast!

WHAT DO YOU CALL A CONVERSATION BETWEEN TWO RUBBISH BAGS?

TRASH TALK!

Plus, the grabby tools were perfect for those hard-to-reach places ...

The rubbish was **REALLY** piling up! And our town was starting to look **SO MUCH BETTER.** It was as neat as a poodle at a wedding!

DON'T TOUCH THE HAIR!

We met some awesome people while we tidied too. Everyone was busier than a **bee in a flower shop!**

We also found some really cool stuff, like this funny hat.

I'LL TAKE THAT HAT FOR A SPIN!

'Better not spin it too fast, or you'll lift off!' said Lizzie.

UP,
UP
AND
AWAAAAAAY!

And Lizzie found a pretty
PAINTING OF A COW!

'That belongs in a **mooooseum!**'
said Kev.

As we were starting to finish up for the day – we found a **pair of glasses** stuck between two big rocks ... They were small, **red**, and looked pretty new.

I BET SOMEONE'S MISSING THOSE ...

Luckily, we had the grabby tools to reach them! **TWO** grabby tools!

I gave the glasses a wipe and popped them in my pocket.

We'd worked so hard tidying up our town
. . . and at the end of the day, we'd filled
a whopping **EIGHT** rubbish bags!

We wheeled them to our front yard and
lined them up.

PHEW!

Would our **STASH OF TRASH** be enough to win us the Jungle trip?! Maybe!

We'd have to wait and see how our bags weighed in at the rubbish dump in the morning!

But for now, we wanted to try and find the owner of the red glasses. We grabbed some cardboard . . .

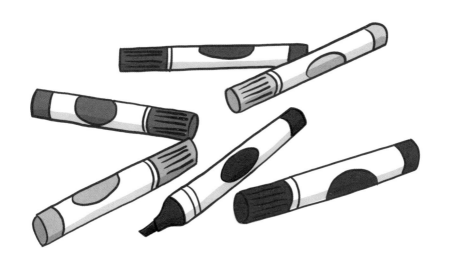

and colourful markers . . .

. . . and drew up some posters.

KEV drew up a great poster with a picture of himself wearing the glasses.

WE FOUND
SOME GLASSES!

My poster had a **HUGE** picture of the glasses.

LOST YOUR GLASSES? COME TO MY
PLACE AND *SEE* WHAT HAPPENS!

And Lizzie's poster was a real **SPECTACLE!**

FOUND: GLASSES. WE'VE EVEN CLEANED THEM SO YOU WON'T GET DIRTY LOOKS!

We took our posters down to 'Percy Pelican's Print Palace' and had copies made. Because it was for a good cause, Percy did it for free!

Then we stuck up posters . . .

PERCY'S PRINT PALACE

ALL over town.

Just as we were heading back home again, a family of cockatoos flew overhead. They called out . . .

'**Hello, Cockatoos!**' we shouted back.

The cockatoos swooped down and landed nearby.

'Our son Colin **lost his glasses** in the bush last week,' said one of the cockatoos.

She pointed her wing to the smallest bird, who was squinting up at us.

'They're red glasses,' the mummy cockatoo continued, 'just like the picture in your posters.'

'Guess who I **bumped** into,' said Colin, 'while searching for my glasses?'

'Who?' I replied.

EVERYBODY!

DONK!

I pulled the glasses out of my pocket
and handed them to Colin.

He popped them on and **BINGO!** He
could see properly again!

I CAN
SEE!

'Thank you!' said Colin, rushing over to give me a hug.

We were so happy to help poor Colin **see** again!

We waved to the cockatoos as they flew away. 'Thanks again, Hotdog!' the daddy cockatoo called out.

We'd had such an awesome day.

Finally, we fell asleep . . . dreaming of winning the contest and **JUNGLE** prize!

TWO

We couldn't WAIT to take our trash to the dump and find out whether we'd collected enough to **win** the Tidy Your Town Day contest!

But when we ran outside . . .

OUR RUBBISH BAGS WERE GONE!

THEY'D VANISHED!

'Do you think it's some sort of magic trick?' asked Kev.

FOR MY NEXT TRICK I'LL MAKE THIS RUBBISH DISAPPEAR!

'I don't think so, Kev. Someone must have **STOLEN** them!' I told him.

'They're trying to pinch that **JUNGLE HOLIDAY** away from us!' added Lizzie.

We'd worked SO hard, and couldn't believe someone would try and take that from us.

SQUAWK!

There was a loud cry from the sky. It was Colin and his family of cockatoos.

They flew down to see what the trouble was.

'What's wrong, Kev?' asked Colin.

'Someone's **stolen** our trash bags!'
Kev howled.

'Unbelievable!' added Mummy
Cockatoo.

LET'S TAKE TO THE SKY AND SEE WHETHER WE CAN SPOT THE CROOKS!

'Let's go!' called Colin. And with that,
the cockatoo family set off to help us
find and rescue those bags!

'They're off to a **flying** start!' said
Lizzie as we watched them circle high
above, searching the streets nearby.

'How will they know where to look?'
asked Kev.

I SUPPOSE
THEY'LL JUST
WING IT!

'While our friends look from the **air**, we should have a look on **ground**!' I said to the gang.

First we went and searched down by the lake. Kev thought he spotted our bags, but it was just some **spotty fish** having a party.

Next, we looked in the **cave** up by the woods. The only thing we found there was a family of bats, and they hadn't seen any rubbish bags.

HEY, WHY DON'T YOU HANG AROUND FOR A WHILE?

We even checked the basement of
Sammy Squirrel's house, who collected
EVERYTHING! We found plenty of
rubbish, but not ours.

We had no luck.

'We're never going to find our bags of rubbish,' moped Kev.

'Don't give up hope, Kev,' I said.

'Don't worry, Kev,' Lizzie said. 'Let's keep looking.'

Just then, we heard a loud **SQUAWK** from up high. It was Colin!

'I've found your rubbish!' said Colin, pointing to his glasses. 'Lucky I've got my glasses back!'

AWESOME!

'Thanks, Colin!' I called out. 'Do you know who took it?!'

'Yeah,' said Lizzie, 'let me at 'em! I'm a lean, mean, lizard machine!'

RUBBISH RASCALS!

'We don't know who they are yet,' said Colin.

'But there's a car that just parked outside a burger shop down the road . . .' said Daddy Cockatoo. 'And your **EIGHT** bags of garbage are in the back!'

We took off after Colin and his family as they led us across town to the **crooks**.

Sure enough, outside the burger shop there was a car with **OUR** spotty orange rubbish bags loaded into the back.

UNBELIEVABLE.

BURGI

Lizzie was ready to run out and rip into the thieves, but Kev held her back.

WHY I OUGHTTA-

'Wait, let's see who's behind this . . .' said Kev.

We waited quietly for the baddies to get out of the car.

Suddenly, the doors opened . . . and out stepped . . .

ROOSTER AND DONKEY!

Those rotten guys had caused so much **trouble** in our town – and they were doing it again!

As soon as they disappeared into the burger shop, we **sprang** into action.

With everyone's help, we snatched all **EIGHT** bags back and bolted outta there before you could say –

COCKADOODLE HEE-HAW!

Our new cockatoo friends were so awesome. They'd asked their friend, Dan Toucan, to bring his van around to help us get on our way in a hurry.

HOP IN!

We hauled the bags into the **Toucan Van** and hit the road.

And as we took off, Rooster and Donkey came running out of the shop.

Thank goodness I'd found Colin's glasses for him – we would **NEVER** have been able to track down those baddies without his super-spotting from the sky!

At the dump, we waited to weigh in our rubbish . . .

Everyone had done such an awesome
job of tidying the town. It was a **HUGE**
effort. Mayor Magpie was so proud, he
couldn't keep the grin off his beak!

BEFORE, OUR TOWN WAS
SHABBY, AND NOW IT'S
SPARKLING!

10 KG

MAYOR

I had a good feeling about our **EIGHT** bags. We had **SO** much rubbish.

And guess what?!

We won!

We had the most rubbish **BY FAR!**

'Congratulations, Hotdog, Lizzie and Kev! Our terrific **Tidy Your Town** winners!' said Mayor Magpie.

And now we were going on a **JUNGLE** adventure!

THREE

I t was **JUNGLE** time! Our safari holiday was finally here . . . and we were super **EXCITED!**

Kev wanted to see some **BIG CATS.**

I couldn't wait to meet an **ELEPHANT.**

Lizzie wanted to see a **giraffe** in the wild.

GREETINGS, YOUR HIGHNESS!

We felt so good after our big clean-up on **Tidy Your Town Day,** that we still took our grabby tools with us everywhere! We couldn't help but **pick up rubbish** everywhere we went.

GOT IT!

Even **ON** the plane!

When we landed, our guide Grace
helped us with our bags and welcomed
us to her hometown . . .

'Home to the best **JUNGLE SAFARI** in
the **WORLD**,' she said. 'You're going to
love it here.'

Grace led us to the airport exit, where a
HUGE T-Rex skeleton loomed above us.
'This is something we're **REALLY** proud
of,' she said, pointing up.

Wow, that dinosaur was massive!

Grace told us how they'd found the
bones not too far away . . . but there was
one problem.

OUR T-REX IS MISSING HIS BIG TOE!

Oh no!

Grace introduced us to the expert on dinosaurs, Dr Taylor Turtle, who found the bones.

'It's the only part we haven't been able
to find,' said Dr Taylor. 'And we have
searched the jungle **HIGH** and **LOW**.'

THAT'S
TOE-TALLY
TERRIBLE!

'One day, it'll show up,' she said,
hopefully, 'and our **T-Rex** will finally be
complete.'

'I reckon you'll find it,' I said, 'I can feel it **IN MY BONES!**'

Grace pointed to a cool jeep waiting outside. 'Over here's your ride,' she said.

'Bye Dr Taylor,' we called.

Grace jumped into the driver's seat and beeped the horn.

'Let's get you to your cabin!' she said.

All three of us piled in. We couldn't wait to check out where we'd be staying!

We made our way up a huge mountain, and soon we were driving along a track through the jungle!

'Welcome!' called out an ostrich pair as they raced alongside our jeep.

IT WAS NECK AND NECK!

Our jungle cabin was in a small clearing, just by a river. It was paradise!

Grace said she'd be back in the morning . . .

And guess what? We had triple bunk beds and hot chocolate waiting for us!

FOUR

It was **JUNGLE SAFARI TIME!**

BEEP!

We set out at sunrise and had our **binoculars** ready for some awesome animal spotting.

'Hey!' said Lizzie. 'I see something already!'

IT'S A BIG CAT!

'Nup, just little old me!' said Kev.

'Oops, I had the binoculars round the wrong way!' said Lizzie.

'Look!' I shouted, spotting something myself. A herd of zebras were making their way across the path ahead.

ZEBRA CROSSING!

It was so cool!

'I wish I looked that good in stripes,' said Lizzie.

WHAT DO YOU THINK?

Just after we passed the herd of zebras, we heard a loud **RUMBLING!**

What could it be?!

We looked around, trying to see what was headed our way.

RHINOS!

'How do you stop a bunch of rhinos from **CHARGING**?!' I shouted.

'Easy,' she said.

I was about to say that this was NOT the time for jokes, when the **rhinos** suddenly swerved and thundered away from us.

'They are SO AMAZING!' cried Lizzie. 'I wish *I* had a rhino horn. Imagine what you could do with one of those?'

Forgot your keys?

Can't find the piñata stick at a party?

SMASH!

Need to crack open a nut?

Jungle animals are **SO** good at hiding, I was having trouble spotting anything!

I saw something big and grey moving in a nearby waterhole.

'**HIPPOS!**' I shouted. 'Over there!'

Grace slowed down our jeep and we all watched the water. There was a whole gang of hippos hanging out.

'What type of music do hippos like?' asked Lizzie. '**Hippo-Hop!**'

'Look!' said Kev. 'That one's opening its mouth!'

We watched the hippo's **enormous jaws** open wide . . .

to our jeep's windscreen!

Our jeep was **COVERED** in hippo snot!

Grace put on the windscreen wipers but they were no match for all that **hippo booger.** We couldn't see a thing!

Luckily, an **ELEPHANT** was nearby and had seen what happened! She dipped her trunk in the waterhole, then blasted that hippo snot right off our jeep!

SPLASH! SWOOSH!

'I'm always **CLEANING UP** after him!' she added.

We'd just seen a hippo sneeze, and now I was meeting a real life **jungle elephant!** I couldn't believe it!

'Thank you!' I called out, and the elephant trumpeted loudly in the air as we continued on our way.

Next, it was Kev's turn to get excited.

'My **MANE MAN!**' he called out,
pointing ahead.

A huge lion sat atop a rock in the sun,
shaking out an incredible mane.

SWISH, SWISH!

'It would be **scary** to be that lion's hairdresser!' said Lizzie.

'Wow,' Kev gasped. 'Oh, I wish I had hair like that!' he added. 'I'd be the **king** of the jungle!'

SWISH, SWISH!

I'M A DANDY LION.

'Give us a **ROAR!**' Kev called out, and
the lion turned towards us and . . .

ROARRRRRR!

'Whoa,' said Kev. 'Big jungle cats are
ROARSOME!'

We continued on our way until we were stopped by a group of **giraffes** on the path ahead. Lizzie practically jumped out of her seat when she saw them!

'WOULD YOU LOOK AT THAT?!' she cried out.

IT'S A GIR-RAFFIC JAM!

'They are amazing,' said Lizzie. 'But I'd feel SO dizzy being up that high!'

MY HEAD IS SPINNING!

'What a pain in the **neck**,' laughed Lizzie.

'Having fun, everyone?' Grace asked.

'Absolutely!' we agreed.

'I'm having more fun than a penguin at a pool party!' said Kev.

'Wonderful,' said Grace. 'There's a perfect **picnic spot** ahead where we can stop in the savannah and have something to eat.'

Our stomachs grumbled at the thought!

FIVE

The picnic spot wasn't too far away from the waterhole.

As we neared it, we could see something strange scattered in the grassland . . .

What was it?

We peered through our binoculars . . .

It was RUBBISH!

People must have been leaving their picnic rubbish behind in the jungle! What **litter bugs**!

In one spot, there was a **huge** mountain of trash. It was almost as tall as me.

'Lunch can wait,' I said, nodding at my friends. I quickly fetched my **grabby tool** and a couple of rubbish bags from my backpack.

WE HAVE CLEANING UP TO DO!

The three of us hopped out of the jeep and got to work. Grace joined us too. **We needed to tidy the jungle!**

We sorted and sifted through the grass, **snatching up rubbish** as quickly as we could.

We also **SPOTTED** some more cool animals.

HOW DO I LOOK IN SPOTS?

We even saw a chimpanzee trading rubbish with a baboon. It looked like some serious **MONKEY BUSINESS!**

Soon, we realised that others were joining in and helping to clean up too!

The jungle was starting to look really good . . .

JUST LIKE IT SHOULD.

Soon, the jungle looked perfect. Clean, green and full of happy wildlife. Not a single piece of rubbish in sight.

I knew we could do it! You can do anything you set your mind to.

IT'S CALLED A RUBBISH *CAN*, NOT A RUBBISH *CANNOT.*

We'd seen so much awesome wildlife. Met great animals. And we even had fun **CLEANING UP!**

This had been the **TRIP** of a lifetime.

What on earth was that?!

'Are you okay?' my friends asked, rushing over to help me up.

I stood up and looked behind me.

Something big and white was sticking out of the ground – in the spot that was covered in a **mountain of trash** not so long ago.

'What is that?' I said, walking over to the **strange object** that had just tripped me. Grace and my friends followed.

I knelt down and started digging. Digging is something I'm **REALLY** good at.

And would you believe what I uncovered?

It was one of the most amazing things I'd ever seen in my **whole entire hotdoggie life!**

SIX

We pulled up at the airport and ran inside with what we'd found.

QUICK!

Our noisy arrival had caused quite a fuss and a whole heap of people had gathered around the **T-Rex** to see whether we'd found the missing piece.

Including Dr Taylor, the dinosaur expert!

COULD IT BE?!

Dr Taylor delicately examined what I'd found. Her eyes were wide and her **smile** grew even wider as she sized everything up.

The crowd suddenly grew quiet.

'Hotdog,' said Dr Taylor, nodding towards the dinosaur's foot.

GO ON, SEE IF IT FITS . . .

We'd found the **BIG TOE!**

The entire airport exploded into cheers!
It was incredible!

'HOTDOG! HOTDOG! HOTDOG!'
they chanted, lifting me and my friends
up on their shoulders.

We felt like *jungle heroes!*

Dr Taylor and Grace gave us a huge hug. 'Thank you SO much!' they gushed.

And guess what? We even made it to the front cover of the **JUNGLE TIMES** newspaper!

What an adventure!

MORE ADVENTURES COMING SOON!

COLLECT THEM WHILE

THEY'RE HOT!